1934
HAPPY BIRTHDAY, KIT!
A Springtime Story

BY VALERIE TRIPP

ILLUSTRATIONS WALTER RANE

VIGNETTES SUSAN McALILEY

American Girl®

Visit our Web site at **americangirl.com**

Printed in China.
02 03 04 05 06 07 08 LEO 12 11 10 9 8 7 6 5 4

The American Girls Collection®, Kit®, Kit Kittredge®, and American Girl®
are registered trademarks of Pleasant Company.

PICTURE CREDITS
The following individuals and organizations have generously given
permission to reprint images contained in "Looking Back":

pp. 64–65—© Bettmann/CORBIS (doctor with baby);
courtesy of the Antoinette Reckwerdt family (couple); © CORBIS (man on road);
pp. 66–67—Franklin D. Roosevelt Library (girl with preserves);
courtesy of J. C. Allen & Son, Inc. (shelling peas, cider making);
courtesy of Mrs. Muriel Church, Kingsley, MI, and Reiman Publishing (feed-sack dresses);
private collection of Mary Louise McDaniel, El Reno, OK (feed-sack dolls);
pp. 68–69—© Bettmann/CORBIS (doctor's office); Franklin D. Roosevelt Library (FDR);
Library of Congress, Prints and Photographs Division (WPA poster);
courtesy of J. C. Allen & Son, Inc. (bookmobile, movie theater);
© Bettmann/CORBIS (family).

Cover Background by Mike Wimmer

Library of Congress Cataloging-in-Publication Data

Tripp, Valerie, 1951–
Happy birthday, Kit! : a springtime story / by Valerie Tripp ;
illustrations, Walter Rane ; vignettes, Susan McAliley.
p. cm. — (The American girls collection)
Summary: On a visit to Cincinnati from rural Kentucky during the Great Depression,
Aunt Millie impresses Kit with her money-saving cleverness.
Includes information on life in America during the Great Depression.
ISBN 1-58485-023-X (hc.) — ISBN 1-58485-022-1 (pbk.)
1. Depressions—1929—Juvenile fiction.
[1. Depressions—1929—Fiction. 2. Aunts—Fiction. 3. Resourcefulness—Fiction.]
I. Rane, Walter, ill. II. McAliley, Susan, ill.
III. American girl (Middleton, Wis.) IV. Title. V. Series.
PZ7.T7363 Haof 2001 [Fic]—dc21 00-047826

FOR TAMARA ENGLAND, SALLY WOOD, AND
JUDY WOODBURN, WITH THANKS

THE AMERICAN GIRLS

17 64

KAYA, an adventurous Nez Perce girl whose deep love
for horses and respect for nature nourish her spirit

17  74

FELICITY, a spunky, spritely colonial girl,
full of energy and independence

18  24

JOSEFINA, an Hispanic girl whose heart and
hopes are as big as the New Mexico sky

18 54

KIRSTEN, a pioneer girl of strength and
spirit who settles on the frontier

18  64

ADDY, a courageous girl determined to be
free in the midst of the Civil War

19  04

SAMANTHA, a bright Victorian beauty, an
orphan raised by her wealthy grandmother

19  34

KIT, a clever, resourceful girl facing the
Great Depression with spirit and determination

19  44

MOLLY, who schemes and dreams on the
home front during World War Two

Table of Contents

DAD
*Kit's father, a
businessman facing
the problems of the
Great Depression.*

MOTHER
*Kit's mother, who takes
care of her family and
their home with strength
and determination.*

KIT
*A clever, resourceful
girl who helps her family
cope with the dark days
of the Depression.*

CHARLIE
*Kit's affectionate
and supportive
older brother.*

**AUNT
MILLIE**
*The lively and loving
woman who raised Dad.*

MRS. HOWARD
*Mother's garden club
friend, who is a guest in
the Kittredge home.*

STIRLING
HOWARD
*Mrs. Howard's son,
whose delicate health
hides surprising
strengths.*

RUTHIE
SMITHENS
*Kit's best friend, who
is loyal, understanding,
and generous.*

ROGER
*A know-it-all boy
in Kit's class.*

ONE

SECRETS AND
SURPRISES

'Spring Arrivals.'

Kit Kittredge grinned at the headline she had typed. **Spring**, she thought. *Now there is a word with some bounce to it.*

It was a sunny Saturday morning in April. Kit was sitting at the desk in her attic room with all the windows wide open to the spring breezes. She and her best friend, Ruthie, were making a newspaper. What Kit was *supposed* to be making was her *bed*, but the newspaper was much more fun. Kit loved to write. She loved to call attention to what was new, or important, or remarkable. So, as often as she could, Kit made a newspaper for everyone in her house to read.

That was quite a few people these days! When Kit's dad lost his job nine months ago because of the Depression, her family turned their home into a boarding house to earn money. Eleven people were living there now. Kit's newspapers were read by her mother, dad, and older brother Charlie, two nurses named Miss Hart and Miss Finney, a musician named Mr. Peck, a friend of Mother's named Mrs. Howard, and her son, Stirling, who was Kit's age. At breakfast this morning, Kit had interviewed Mr. and Mrs. Bell, an elderly couple who had just moved in. Now she was writing an article about them to help everyone else get to know them.

'Let's all wellcome Mr. and Mrs. Bell,' Kit typed. She stopped. "Hey, Ruthie," she asked, "does *welcome* have one **l** or two?"

Ruthie started to answer. But suddenly, a gust of wind blew in through the window, swooped up all the papers on Kit's desk, and sent them flying around the room like gigantic, clumsy butterflies. Ruthie and Kit both yelped. They sprang up to chase the papers and heard someone laughing.

It was Stirling. "Close the windows!" he said.

"Too late for that," said Kit, laughing with him.

By now the papers had fluttered to the floor. Kit and Ruthie and Stirling knelt down to collect them.

Stirling held up a page that had been cut from a magazine. "What's this?" he asked.

"Nothing!" said Kit, snatching it away.

"Nothing?" asked Stirling, in his voice that was surprisingly low for someone so little and skinny.

"Well," said Kit, "it's . . . a secret."

"Oh," said Stirling and Ruthie together.

Kit thought quickly. Her friends were good at keeping secrets—this she knew for sure. They were trustworthy, and they'd never laugh at her. She decided to let them in on her secret. "Promise you won't tell," she said.

"I promise," said Ruthie, crossing her heart.

"Me, too," said Stirling.

Kit stood next to them so that they could all look at the magazine page together. "It's a picture of a birthday party for a movie star's child," she said. "See? Some of the kids are riding horses, and some are playing with bows and arrows, and they're all dressed like characters from *Robin Hood*."

"Your favorite book," said Ruthie. "Oh, I *love* this picture!"

"Look in the trees," Kit said enthusiastically. "There are ropes so the kids can swing from tree to tree like Robin and his men. And there are tree houses on different branches. There's even one at the top of the tree, like the tower of a castle. Some of the kids are eating birthday cake up there."

"Wow," said Stirling quietly. He looked at Kit. His gray eyes were serious. "I think I know why this is a secret," he said. "Because—"

"Because my birthday is coming up in May and I don't want my parents to know that I'd love to have a party like this one!" Kit burst out. "It would only make them feel bad. I know they hate always having to say that we don't have enough money."

Ruthie looked sorry, and Stirling nodded. Kit was sure they understood. They both knew that the Kittredges were just scraping by. If Mr. Kittredge's Aunt Millie had not sent them money, the Kittredges would have been evicted from their house right after Christmas because they couldn't pay the bank what they owed for the mortgage.

Kit took one last longing look at the picture,

folded it carefully, and put it away in her desk drawer. "Don't forget you promised not to tell anyone my secret," she said. "Especially not my mother. She's so busy now that she has to cook and clean for eleven people." Kit sighed. "I know I can't have a party like the one in the picture. I shouldn't *really* want any party at all. But I can't help it. I do."

"I think," Stirling said slowly, "that it's okay to want something, even if it seems impossible. Isn't that the same as hoping?"

"That's right," said Ruthie. "And hope is always good. If we just give up on everything, how will anything ever get better?"

"Hope is always good," Kit repeated. She grinned and tilted her head toward the drawer where the picture of the party was hidden. "Even," she said, "if it has to be secret."

Ruthie went home, and Kit put Stirling to work drawing a mitt, bat, cap, and ball to go with an article she'd written for her newspaper about the Cincinnati Reds, the baseball team she and Stirling liked best. While he drew, Kit went to work herself.

She took the sheets off her bed. She was careful not to tear them. They were worn so thin that she could almost see through the middles! But there was no money to buy new sheets, and what good sheets there were had to be saved for the boarders' beds.

"See you later," she said to Stirling as she carried the sheets downstairs.

"Okay," said Stirling, busy drawing.

Every Saturday, it was Kit's job to change the sheets on all the beds. She gathered up the used sheets, washed, dried, and ironed them, then remade the beds with clean sheets. Miss Hart and Miss Finney always left their sheets in a neatly folded bundle next to the laundry tubs, and Mrs. Howard was so persnickety that she insisted on doing all of her laundry herself. Even so, by the time Kit had gathered the rest of the sheets and pillowcases this morning, the pile was so big that she could hardly see over the top of it. She couldn't help feeling exasperated when, as she headed to the laundry tubs in the basement, the doorbell rang.

"I'll get it!" she called. Kit waddled to the door and fumbled with the knob. The sheets began to fall,

so she hooked her foot around the door to swing it
open. When she saw who was standing outside, Kit
dropped the pile of sheets and flung her arms open
wide. "Aunt Millie!" she cried as she plunged into a
hug. "What a great surprise!"

"Margaret Mildred Kittredge," said Aunt Millie,
using Kit's whole name. "Let me look at you."
She stepped back and eyed Kit from head to toe.
"Heavenly day!" she exclaimed. "You've sprung up
like a weed! You must be two feet taller than you
were when I saw you last July! And still the prettiest
child there ever was! It's worth the trip from
Kentucky just to see you."

"I'm glad to see you, too," said Kit, practically
dancing with excitement as she led Aunt Millie
inside. "I didn't know you were coming."

"No one did," said Aunt Millie. "I just took it
into my head to come, and here I am, blown in on
the breeze like a bug. Now where are your dad and
mother? And where's your handsome brother?"

"Charlie's at work, but he'll be home soon," said
Kit. "Mother and Dad are cleaning out the garage.
We're so crowded in the house now with all the
boarders, we need room out there for storage."

As Kit spoke, Aunt Millie put her suitcase and basket in the corner. She took off her hat and coat, put her gloves in her purse, and hung her things neatly on a hook in the hall. She turned and saw the pile of sheets Kit had dropped. "Changing sheets today, are we?" she observed. "Odd to do it on Saturday, with everyone underfoot. Still, it's a good drying day today." She scooped up half the pile. "We'd better begin."

"But Aunt Millie," said Kit as she picked up the rest of the sheets. "Don't you want to say hello to Mother and Dad first?"

"Time enough for that after we get the laundry started," said Aunt Millie. "Work before pleasure. Come along, Margaret Mildred. If we dillydally, we'll waste the best sunshine."

Kit grinned. *That's Aunt Millie for you,* she thought. *Never wastes a thing, not even sunshine.*

Aunt Millie was not really Kit's aunt, or Dad's either. Mother said that calling her "Aunt" when she was no relation was a very countrified thing to do, and that they should call her "Miss Mildred" because it showed more respect. But Aunt Millie pooh-poohed putting on such airs. "Call me anything, except late for dinner," she'd say. And so "Aunt Millie" she remained. Besides, she and her husband, Birch, were the only family Dad had ever known. They had adopted Dad after his parents died when he was a boy. Uncle Birch worked in the coal mine in Mountain Hollow, Kentucky, until he died. Kit's family visited Aunt Millie there every Fourth of July. But Aunt Millie never came to Cincinnati. "Too many people, not enough animals," she always said. So this visit was a big surprise.

"I can't wait till Mother and Dad see you!" said Kit as she put the sheets in sudsy water to soak. "They'll be so glad you've come for a visit."

"Out of the blue," said Aunt Millie. She smoothed her dress, straightened her shoulders, and smiled at Kit. "'Lead on, Macduff!'" she said, pointing up the basement stairs. Kit was used to the way Aunt Millie quoted poetry and Shakespeare right in the middle of a normal conversation. Aunt Millie had been the schoolteacher in Mountain Hollow ever since Uncle Birch died, and she couldn't stop herself from teaching wherever she was.

William Shakespeare

"I can't wait till Mother and Dad see you!" said Kit.

The sunshine was dazzling after the dimness of the basement. Kit squinted and Aunt Millie shaded her eyes as they crossed the yard. "Mother and Dad!" Kit called. "Come see our surprise!"

Mother and Dad came out of the garage blinking from the brightness and from amazement.

"Aunt Millie!" Dad exclaimed, striding forward to hug her. "How wonderful! I'm glad to see you!"

"I'm glad to see you, too!" Aunt Millie said.

"Miss Mildred, we're honored," said Mother. "It's so kind of you to make the trip. You look well."

"Fit as a fiddle," said Aunt Millie. "And—"

"—twice as stringy," she and Dad finished together.

Dad threw back his head and laughed with Aunt Millie at their old joke. Kit beamed. It'd been a long time since she'd heard Dad laugh so heartily. No one could make him laugh the way Aunt Millie could!

"I never thought I'd see the day you'd leave your home and come to the city," Dad said to Aunt Millie. "How's everybody in Mountain Hollow?"

"We've been through hard times before," said Aunt Millie. "We'll make it through this rough

11

patch. But the town's been hit pretty badly by this Depression. Last week, they closed the mine. Just couldn't make any money from it. When they shut the mine, they closed down the school, and of course my house went with my job, so I lost *it*, too."

"Oh, no!" exclaimed Dad, Mother, and Kit.

But Aunt Millie did not sound the least bit sorry for herself. "My friend Myrtle Peabody's been after me for years to live with her," she said. "So I guess that's what I'll do." She smiled at Kit and tousled her hair. "I just thought I'd come and see how you folks are doing for a while first."

"You are very welcome," said Dad. "Stay as long as you like."

"Yes," said Mother. "You'll stay in our room while you're here. Kit can take you there now for a rest. You must be tired from traveling."

"Heavenly day, Margaret!" said Aunt Millie. "I'm not the least bit tired. And you needn't treat *me* like company. I wouldn't dream of taking your room. I can park my bones anyplace. Just put me in a corner somewhere."

"Dear me, no!" said Mother. She smiled, but Kit saw she was worried.

Poor Mother! thought Kit. *She wants to make Aunt Millie comfortable, but we don't have a room to put her in. The house is full of boarders.*

"Aunt Millie can share with me," Kit offered. "There's plenty of room in my attic, and an extra bed we can set up, too."

"That'll be jim-dandy," said Aunt Millie.

"I guess it'll do," said Mother, "since it's just for a while."

"Come on, Aunt Millie," said Kit, taking her hand. "I'll show you the attic. You can meet Stirling. He's up there now drawing illustrations for our newspaper." She grinned. "After I finish the laundry, I'll write an article about you!"

Stirling and Aunt Millie liked each other right away. Aunt Millie was a Cincinnati Reds fan, too. When she praised Stirling's baseball drawings, he turned bright pink with pride.

After Stirling left, Aunt Millie said to Kit, "That boy's as scrawny as a plucked chicken now. But you mark my words—he'll grow into that voice and those ears and elbows someday. And when he does, he'll be a handsome fellow."

Kit giggled at the impossible thought of pip-squeaky Stirling ever being handsome. But Aunt Millie had a way of seeing the potential in people and bringing out the best in them, too.

At first, when Dad introduced her to all the boarders at dinner, everyone was shy. They didn't know quite what to make of Aunt Millie, with her wispy white hair, her cheeks as red as scrubbed apples, her twangy Kentucky accent, her funny expressions, and her quotes that sprang out unexpectedly.

When Aunt Millie passed Mr. Peck the mashed potatoes, she said, "Here, son. You've got that 'lean and hungry look.'"

Mr. Peck smiled, but he looked bewildered. So did almost everyone else.

"That's a quote from Shakespeare," Kit explained.

"*Julius Caesar,*" said Aunt Millie. She turned to Mr. and Mrs. Bell. "Didn't I read in Kit's newspaper that you've acted in some of Shakespeare's plays?"

"Indeed, we have!" said Mr. Bell.

"Please tell us about it," said Aunt Millie, looking very interested.

Mrs. Bell told a funny story about Mr. Bell tripping over his sword in a play. That reminded Mr. Peck of the time three strings on his bass fiddle popped during a concert. And *that* reminded Miss Finney of a patient who was an opera singer and sang whenever he called for her. Soon everyone was telling funny stories and laughing uproariously—even Mrs. Howard, whose usual laugh was just a nervous giggle. Aunt Millie's contagious hoot was loudest of all.

Kit looked at Aunt Millie and grinned from ear to ear. *When I wrote my headline this morning,* Kit thought, *I never guessed who the very best and most surprising spring arrival of all would be!*

CHAPTER

TWO

—

THE WASTE-NOT,
WANT-NOT
ALMANAC

The next day, Aunt Millie woke Kit
early. "Come with me," she said.
"Now?" Kit asked groggily.
"Yes! Time to greet the 'rosy-fingered dawn,'"
Aunt Millie replied.

Kit swung out of bed and dressed as quickly
as she could. She saw that Aunt Millie was not
wearing the Sunday-best clothes she had worn
for traveling the day before. Instead, she was
wearing no-nonsense work clothes. Her old
leather boots had seen better days, her straw
hat looked chewed, and her sweater had mis-
matched buttons and tidy patches on the elbows.
Over her faded, but very clean, flowered dress,

she wore a starched and ironed all-over
apron. She was holding two empty cloth
sacks in her hand.

"What're we doing?" Kit whispered
as she tiptoed behind Aunt Millie.

"Collecting while the dew is fresh,"
said Aunt Millie. When they were outside, Aunt
Millie handed Kit one of the sacks. "We're going to
gather dandelion greens for salad," she said.

"Dandelions?" squeaked Kit. "You mean we're
going to eat our lawn?"

Aunt Millie picked out a dandelion green and
handed it to Kit. "Taste this," she said.

Kit took a nibble. "Hey!" she said. "It's good!"

"And free," said Aunt Millie. "Let's get to work."

It was just like Aunt Millie to see the
possibilities in a weed. *No one in the world is better
at making something out of nothing,* Kit thought
as she picked.

By the time everyone else was up,
Aunt Millie and Kit had filled their sacks with
dandelion greens and had also weeded most of
the lawn while they were at it. Aunt Millie was a
great one for being efficient. That very afternoon,

Aunt Millie, Kit, Dad, and Charlie took hoes and shovels out of the garage and started to rip up a corner of the lawn to plant vegetables there.

"Wait!" cried Mother. "I like the idea of growing vegetables. But couldn't we put the patch behind the garage, where people wouldn't see it?"

"This is nice, flat land that gets plenty of sunshine," said Aunt Millie positively. "Things'll grow beautifully here. It's too shady behind the garage."

"I guess that makes sense," said Mother. Kit could tell that Mother was not pleased to have the lawn torn up right next to her azaleas. The plot for the vegetable garden *was* an unsightly mud patch. Kit

azaleas

herself was doubtful that the little seeds Aunt Millie had brought would amount to anything. The seeds were wrapped in twists of newspaper that Aunt Millie had labeled and packed carefully in an old cloth flour sack. As Kit planted the tiny gray seeds, she couldn't believe they'd become big, red tomatoes, orange carrots, green beans, or yellow squash. But Aunt Millie was cheerfully confident that time, sun, water, and hard work would bring

"This is nice, flat land that gets plenty of sunshine," said Aunt Millie positively. "Things'll grow beautifully here."

about the magical transformation.

"How come you're so sure?" Kit asked her.

Aunt Millie considered Kit's question. "I guess teachers and gardeners are just naturally optimistic," she said. "Can't help it. Children and seeds are never disappointing." She stood and brushed the dirt off her knees. "Save the flour sack," she said. "I'll make you a pair of bloomers out of it."

flour-sack bloomers

"Bloomers?" laughed Kit. "Oh, Aunt Millie, you're kidding! I couldn't wear underwear made out of a flour sack, for heaven's sake!"

"And why not?" Aunt Millie asked.

"Well," Kit sputtered, "what if someone saw them? I'd be—"

"Waste not, want not, my girl," said Aunt Millie tartly. Then, like the spring sun coming out from behind a cloud, she smiled. "You'll like the bloomers," she said. "You'll be surprised."

❧

Kit soon learned that life with Aunt Millie around was *full* of surprises because Aunt Millie was full of ingenious ideas. She could find a use for *anything,* even things that were old and worn out. To Aunt Millie, nothing was beyond hope.

"There's plenty of good left in these sheets," she said when Kit showed her the ones that were thin in the middle. It was a few nights later. Everyone was gathered around the radio waiting for President Roosevelt, who was going to speak in what he called a "fireside chat." Aunt Millie was a big fan of President Roosevelt and his wife, Eleanor, and had asked Dad to move Mother's sewing machine into the living room so that she could sew while she listened. She liked to do two things at once.

radio

"Watch this, Margaret Mildred," she said to Kit. As Kit watched, Aunt Millie tore the sheets in half, right down the middle. Then she sewed the outside edges together. "Now the worn parts are on the edges and the good parts are in the middle," she said. "These sheets'll last ten more years."

The next night, Aunt Millie taught Kit how to take the collars and cuffs off Dad's shirts and sew them back on reversed, so that the frayed part was hidden. Kit was pleased to know how to do something so useful. She was glad when Aunt Millie promised, "Tomorrow night I'll teach you how to sew patches on so they don't show." And Kit was proud when, as everyone was saying good night, Aunt Millie announced, "If you've got anything that needs patching, bring it down tomorrow. Margaret Mildred and I'll take care of it for you."

Kit saw that Mother's lips were thin as she tidied up the room. Kit was puzzled. Since Dad lost his job, no one had struggled harder than Mother to save money. Surely she appreciated all Aunt Millie's frugal know-how! And yet it seemed that Mother felt the same way about the sewing machine in the

living room as she'd felt about the vegetable patch in the yard. It was just too visible.

But Kit thought it was great fun to have Aunt Millie and the sewing machine right in the thick of things. The living room felt cheery and cozy in the evenings with the sewing machine clicking away while the boarders chatted or listened to the radio. Kit liked learning all of Aunt Millie's skillful tricks, like how to use material from inside a pocket to lengthen pants, how to embroider yarn flowers over tears,

darning a sock

holes, and stains, and how to darn socks so
that they were as good as new. Aunt Millie
was a good teacher. She was brisk and precise,
but patient.

"I love the way Aunt Millie takes things
that are ugly and used up and changes them into
things that are beautiful and useful," Kit said to
Ruthie and Stirling as they walked home from
school one day.

"Just like Cinderella's fairy godmother," said
Ruthie, who liked fairy tales. "You know, how she
turned Cinderella's rags into a ball gown."

"Aunt Millie uses hard work instead of a wand,"
said Kit. "But it does seem like she can do magic."

"Maybe you should show her the picture of the
Robin Hood party," said Ruthie. "Maybe she could
figure out a way to do that."

"I don't think so," sighed Kit. "But she sure has
lots of great ideas." Suddenly Kit had a great idea of
her own. "You know what we can do?" she said
excitedly. "We can write down Aunt Millie's ideas.
We'll make a book! Ruthie, you and I can write it,
and Stirling can draw the pictures."

"What'll we call it?" asked Ruthie.

"*Aunt Millie's Waste-Not, Want-Not Almanac*," Kit said with a grin. "What else? The thing Aunt Millie hates most is waste, and it would be a terrible waste if we forgot all she's taught us after she leaves. Writing her ideas down will be a way of saving them. We won't tell Aunt Millie about our book. Then right before she goes home, we'll show her. It'll be a way to thank her."

"Is she leaving soon?" asked Stirling.

"I hope not!" said Kit. "Come on, let's run home and get started before I have to do my chores!"

Kit didn't have a blank book, so she took one of Charlie's old composition books, turned it upside down, and wrote on the unused backsides of the pages. She divided *Aunt Millie's Waste-Not, Want-Not Almanac* into four sections: "Growing," "Sewing," "Cooking," and "Miscellaneous Savings." In the "Growing" section, Stirling drew a sketch of the vegetable patch. Ruthie labeled the rows, and Kit wrote Aunt Millie's advice about planting, watering, and weeding in the margins. In the "Sewing" section, Stirling drew diagrams to show how to turn sheets sides-to-middle and how to reverse cuffs. Kit wrote out the directions in easy-to-follow steps.

Almost every day there was something new to add to the *Almanac*. Aunt Millie taught the children how to trace a shoe on a piece of cardboard, cut it out, and put the cardboard in the shoe to cover up a hole in the bottom. She showed them how to take slivers of soap, melt them together, and mold them into new bars of soap. She also taught the children to save string, basting thread, and buttons, and to be on the lookout for glass bottles to return for the deposit.

One day, when Kit and Stirling came home from school, they saw a horse-drawn wagon parked in front of the house. It belonged to the ragman, who paid by the pound for cloth rags. Kit had always wanted to get to know the ragman's horse, but Mother never asked the ragman to stop. She said the horse was unsanitary. Aunt Millie, however, was petting the horse and feeding it apple cores. Kit and Stirling were tickled when Aunt Millie let them feed the horse, too.

"'My kingdom for a horse,'" said Aunt Millie, quoting Shakespeare as she petted the horse's nose. She smiled at the ragman.

"If I'd known you were coming, I'd have gathered up some rags to sell you. We have some dandies."

The ragman was very pleased by Aunt Millie's kindness to his horse. "I'll tell you what," he said. "I wasn't planning to come back this way next week, but for you, I will."

Kit and Stirling exchanged a glance. Here was a typical Aunt Millie idea to put in their *Almanac:* save apple cores, charm the ragman, and get good money for your rags!

Saturday rolled around, and Kit was delighted when Aunt Millie announced that she and Kit would do the grocery shopping. They set forth after Kit had washed and ironed all the sheets and remade all the beds. Aunt Millie had her hat firmly fixed on her head and her shopping list, written on the back of an old envelope, firmly held in her hand. Kit skipped along next to Aunt Millie, eager and alert. She was sure to hear more good ideas for the *Almanac* on this shopping trip. Kit had noticed before that when she was writing about something, she had to be especially observant. Writers had to pay attention. Everything *mattered.*

Kit's heart sank a little when she saw that they

were headed to the butcher shop. The butcher was well known to be a stingy grouch.

"What would you like today?" he asked Kit and Aunt Millie.

Aunt Millie spoke with more of a twang than usual. "I'd like," she said, "to know what an old Kentucky hilljack like you is doing in Cincinnati."

Kit gasped. She was sure the butcher would be angry. It was not complimentary to call someone a "hilljack." But Aunt Millie's question seemed to have worked another one of her magical transformations.

Smiling, the butcher asked, "How'd you know I'm from Kentucky?"

"Because your accent's the same as mine," said Aunt Millie.

The butcher laughed. For a long while, he and Aunt Millie chatted and swapped jokes as if they were old friends.

"Now," Aunt Millie said at last, "if you've got a soup bone and some meat scraps you could let me have for a nickel, I'll make some of my famous soup." She pointed to Kit. "And Margaret Mildred here will bring you a portion. How's that?"

"It's a deal," said the butcher cheerfully.

As they left the butcher shop, Kit hefted the heavy parcel of meat. "Gosh, Aunt Millie," she said. "All this for a nickel?"

"A nickel and some friendliness," Aunt Millie said. "Works every time." She caught Kit's arm. "Slow down there, child. What's your hurry?"

"Well," said Kit, "you and the butcher talked so long, I'm afraid the grocery store will be closing when we get there."

Aunt Millie winked. "I hope so," she said.

Kit was confused until Aunt Millie explained,

"Tomorrow's Sunday and the store'll be closed. So, just before closing time today, the grocer will lower the prices on things that'll go bad by Monday."

"Ah! I see!" said Kit.

Of course, Aunt Millie was right. The grocer *was* lowering the prices. Aunt Millie and Kit were able to get wonderful bargains on vegetables close to wilting, fruit that was at its ripest, and bread about to go stale. Aunt Millie bought a whole bag of day-old rolls, jelly buns, and doughnuts for a dime, a loaf of crushed bread and a box of broken cookies for a nickel each, two dented cans of peaches for six cents, and a huge bag of bruised apples for a quarter.

Kit was impressed by Aunt Millie's money-saving cleverness. Yet for some reason, Kit squirmed. *Everyone in this store must know my family's too poor to pay full prices,* she thought. Aunt Millie counted every penny of her change. When the grocer sighed impatiently and the people waiting in line craned their heads around to see what was taking so long, Kit went hot with self-consciousness.

As they walked home, Aunt Millie said, "You're very quiet, Margaret Mildred. Where's what Shakespeare would call my 'merry lark'?"

Kit spoke slowly. "Aunt Millie," she said, "do you ever feel funny about . . . you know . . . having to buy crushed bread and broken cookies and all?"

"Everything we bought's perfectly good," said Aunt Millie. "It may not *look* perfect, but none of it's rotten or spoiled. It'll taste fine, you'll see."

"I meant," Kit faltered, "it's . . . hard to be poor in front of people."

"Being poor is nothing to be ashamed of," said Aunt Millie stoutly, "especially these days, with so many folks in the same boat."

Kit shook herself. How silly she was being! Of course Aunt Millie was right. Kit knew she should be proud of Aunt Millie's thrifty ideas. Wasn't that the whole point of the *Almanac*? Kit turned her thoughts to her book. *Which section should I put these new grocery shopping ideas in?* she wondered. *"Cooking" or "Miscellaneous Savings"?*

CHAPTER
THREE
—

GRACE

"Guess what?" Stirling asked Kit one afternoon as she was scouring out the bathtub. "We're going to have to add a new section to the *Almanac*."

"What'll it be?" asked Kit.

"Come downstairs," Stirling said, smiling. "You'll see."

Kit finished her cleaning and then went downstairs. The front door was open. Mother, Dad, Stirling, and Aunt Millie were standing outside, gathered around a wooden crate.

Dad grinned at Aunt Millie. "You've outdone yourself this time," he said.

Kit gasped. The crate was full of chickens! Live,

squawking, white-feathered chickens! Kit knelt next to the crate. "Are they ours?" she asked.

"Yes, ma'am," said Aunt Millie. "I swapped for them. Remember that bag of apples? I cut out the bruises, made pies, and traded them."

"You swapped pies for chickens?" asked Dad.

"Well, I threw in a few other things, too," said Aunt Millie.

"Are we . . . are we going to *eat* the chickens?" asked Kit, who had already fallen in love with the fat, noisy, *cluck-cluck-clucking* birds.

"Heavens no!" said Aunt Millie. "We're going to sell their eggs."

"*Who's* going to sell their eggs?" asked Mother.

Aunt Millie put one hand on Kit's shoulder and the other on Stirling's shoulder. "My partners here," she said, "will go door-to-door selling the eggs."

Mother looked dismayed. "The children will be selling eggs to our neighbors?" she asked. "As if they were . . . *peddlers*?"

"Folks are always glad to buy fresh eggs," said Aunt Millie. She turned to Kit and Stirling. "Come on, partners. Let's get these hens settled. The sooner they are settled, the sooner they'll lay eggs, and the sooner we'll be in business."

Stirling looked sideways at Kit. "'Chickens,'" he murmured.

Kit grinned and nodded. That would be the name of the newest section of *Aunt Millie's Waste-Not, Want-Not Almanac.*

Dad built a chicken coop behind the garage. Mother had put her foot down and insisted that the chicken coop must not be visible from the house. Of course, it was still possible to hear and often *smell* the chickens from the house. Kit knew that this distressed Mother, who was not happy about the chickens in the first place. Kit heard her say to Dad, "I do wish Miss Mildred had asked us before she hatched this chickens-and-eggs idea."

Everyone else was delighted with the chickens, especially Kit herself. The chickens weren't very smart, but they were cheerful. They made Kit laugh the way they clucked so excitedly all day long. Kit enjoyed feeding them. She scooped out handfuls of feed from the big cloth feed sack and scattered it on the ground. Often, as she fed the chickens, Kit felt like a farm girl living out in the country long, long ago.

Sometimes it seemed to Kit that she was leading two completely different lives. One life was at home with Aunt Millie and her quirky, economical, country ways that Kit wrote about in the *Almanac*. Her other life, at school, was entirely separate. Except for Ruthie and Stirling, none of Kit's classmates knew anything about her "waste-not, want-not" life at home. Kit wondered what they'd think if they did.

The weather, in spring's fickle way, turned cold and rainy. The rain was good news for the vegetable patch, which had a crew cut of green sprouts. But it was not good news for Kit and Stirling, who were planning to go on their very first egg-selling expedition this very afternoon. The rain was not good news for Mother and Mrs. Howard, either, because for the first time in a long time, the garden club ladies were coming for a meeting.

Inviting the garden club ladies had been another of Aunt Millie's ideas. Mother was reluctant. She liked things to be *just so* for the garden club meetings. Of course, there had been no money or time for such fussing since Dad lost his job and the boarders arrived. The meetings could never again be as fancy or elaborate as those in the old days. For one thing, Mother had sold a great deal of her good silver. But Aunt Millie had insisted they could still have a fine party. "You leave it to me," she had said. "I'll use energy instead of money."

And sure enough, when Kit saw the room set up for the party, she knew that Aunt Millie had pulled off another one of her amazing surprises. She had washed the best linen tablecloth and napkins to make them dazzling white, then starched and ironed them into stiff perfection. She had polished the one remaining silver candleholder until it gleamed. She made peach pies and apple pies that were works of art. No one would know the peaches came out of dented cans and the apples were bruised. And no one would ever guess that her dainty tea sandwiches were made of crushed bread with the crusts cut off and wilted watercress she'd made crisp by soaking it in cold water overnight. Aunt Millie had dusted, polished, and swept the house till it shone, despite the gloomy weather outside.

Mother and Mrs. Howard, who was quite perked up by the idea of the party, placed a gorgeous bouquet of irises from the garden on the table. Then Mother stood back to survey the whole room.

"Miss Mildred," said Mother with a big, genuine smile. "Thank you very much for everything you've done. It all looks beautiful."

"It's just a matter of making the best of what you've got," said Aunt Millie. She shooed Mother out of the room, saying, "You skedaddle now. Go get *yourself* beautiful for your ladies." Then Aunt Millie turned to Kit and Stirling. "You two skedaddle, too. Go sell those eggs. When you're done, come see me. I'll have some goodies for you from the party."

So Kit and Stirling went out into the rain. Kit pulled the wagon while Stirling kept an eye on the eggs. Aunt Millie had divided them into groups of six, which she had wrapped carefully in newspaper so that they wouldn't crack or break. It was raining so hard that the newspaper was soon soggy. Kit tried not to jiggle the wagon as they walked around the corner and up the sidewalk to the first house.

Kit rang the doorbell.

"Yes?" asked the lady who came to the door.

"Would you like to buy some eggs?" Kit asked.

"How much . . . ?" the lady began. She stopped and stared at Kit. "Why, aren't you the little Kittredge girl, Margaret Kittredge's daughter?" she asked, peering through the rain. "What are *you* doing selling eggs? Wherever did you get them?"

The lady's questions embarrassed Kit. She swallowed hard and said, "They're from our chickens. They're twenty-five cents a dozen."

"*Your* chickens?" asked the lady. "It's come to that? Your family is raising chickens? In your yard?"

Kit felt hot, the way she had in the grocery store. The lady made it sound as if her family had lost all dignity and sunk into humiliating poverty.

Stirling glanced at Kit, then saved the situation by speaking up boldly. "Yes, the chickens live right around the corner," he said. "So you know these eggs are good and fresh. How many do you want?"

"Well!" said the lady. "I'll take a dozen." She carefully counted out her money, took the eggs, and closed the door.

Kit turned to Stirling. "Let's go to a street farther away," she said.

"Okay," said Stirling. Kit could tell by the look in his gray eyes that he knew why she wanted to go where no one knew her.

It was easy to sell the eggs, just as Aunt Millie had said it would be. People were pleased to buy fresh eggs delivered right to their doors at a price slightly lower than the price in the store. Kit soon had one dollar and twenty-five cents in her pocket. And yet, as she and Stirling walked home, Kit felt tired and disheartened. She knew she shouldn't have been ashamed by the first lady's questions, but she was, all the same. A drop of rain dripped off the end of her nose. Kit swiped it with her hand, which was also wet. Everything was miserable and discouraging because of the leaden sky and dreary rain. Then, on the sidewalk ahead, Kit saw a muddy brown lump. She stopped.

"What is it?" asked Stirling.

Kit knelt down next to the lump. "It's a dog," she said, gently touching one wet, furry ear. "A poor, starving, pitiful dog." Attached to a string around the dog's neck was a soggy piece of paper with a message on it. The rain had blurred the writing so that the words had inky tears dripping from them, but Kit could read: *Can't feed her any more.*

The dog sighed, and looked at Kit with the saddest eyes she'd ever seen. The look went straight to Kit's heart, making her forget all about her own hurt feelings. "Stirling, this dog's been abandoned," she said. "We've got to bring her home and feed her."

Stirling didn't hesitate. "Let's put her in the wagon," he said. "Aunt Millie will know how to save her."

"Come on, old girl," Kit said softly as she and Stirling awkwardly lifted the dog into the wagon. The poor creature looked like a bag of bones and fur with its short hind legs folded beneath its stomach, its long, forlorn face resting on its muddy front paws, and its droopy ears puddled around its head. The dog did not move or whimper the whole time Kit pulled the wagon home. It did not even lift its head when Kit stopped outside the screen door.

Stirling went into the kitchen and brought Aunt Millie outside.

"You've got to help, Aunt Millie," said Kit. "We think she's starving."

"Heavenly day!" said Aunt Millie. She bent down to examine the dog. "You children did the

"Stirling, this dog's been abandoned," Kit said.

right thing, rescuing this poor dog. She's a sorrowful sight now, and I don't suppose she'll ever be a beauty, but she's a fine old hound. Not a thing wrong with her that food and loving care won't cure. She'll be a good guard dog for us and will more than earn her keep." Aunt Millie stood up and said briskly, "Put her in the garage. Keep her there until your mother's party is over. I'll rustle up some scraps and bring them out to you as soon as I can. Later, we'll bathe her."

As Kit and Stirling pulled the wagon to the garage, several things happened at once. The rain stopped, the clouds parted, and the sun shone at last. Mother and the garden club ladies came outside. They stood on the terrace to admire the azaleas, which looked heavenly with the raindrops sparkling on their delicate, colorful petals. The chickens were drawn outside by the sunshine, too. They emerged from their coop, strutting and clucking with enthusiasm, to peck in the mud for worms brought up by the rain.

At the sound of the chickens, the dog suddenly lifted its nose and sniffed the air. To Kit and Stirling's astonishment, the dog threw back its head and let loose a bloodcurdling howl. The ladies screeched, the chickens squawked, and the dog bolted out of the wagon and took off toward the chickens like a shot, barking wildly. Its lope was ungainly and awkward, but it was amazingly fast. Before anyone knew what was happening, the dog had chased some of the chickens across the lawn and onto the terrace, right into the middle of the ladies! The ladies protested as loudly as the chickens as the dog herded them all into the dining room, closely followed by Kit and Stirling.

Feathers flew. Kit chased the chickens and the dog around the tea table, trying to call to the dog above the ladies' shrieks. Dad, Charlie, and some of the boarders thundered down the stairs shouting, "What's going on?" Aunt Millie heard the racket and barreled out of the kitchen, flapping her apron at the chickens and shouting instructions to Kit.

Finally, Kit took a flying leap and tackled the dog. In so doing, she jostled the table. The china rattled like chattering teeth. The centerpiece of flowers rocked wildly. The candleholder tottered, fell over, then crashed to the floor. Somehow, Aunt Millie and

Stirling shooed the chickens, who were
still clucking indignantly, outside. Kit
dragged the dog into the kitchen. She
didn't dare take it outside until the chickens
were safely shut up in their coop.

The calamity was over, but the party was
ruined. The ladies scooped up their gloves and
purses, said hurried thank-yous and good-byes to
Mother, and scurried home. The house was
suddenly quiet.

"I'm so sorry," said Kit when Mother came into
the kitchen.

"You should apologize to Miss Mildred," said
Mother wearily. "She's the one who worked so hard
to make the party beautiful." Mother shook her
head. "For myself, I don't know whether to laugh or
cry. I've never seen such a disaster in all my life.
Where on earth did that filthy dog come from?"

"Aunt Millie says—" Kit began, but Mother held
up her hand.

"Stop," she said. "Don't bother telling me. I can
guess. The dog is one of Miss Mildred's rescue
projects." She sighed. "I am grateful for all her hard
work these past weeks. But I'm at my wit's end! My

home has not been my own since . . ." Mother didn't finish her sentence, but she didn't need to. Kit knew that she was going to say "since Miss Mildred came."

Mother put her hands on her hips and leaned forward. "You," she said to the dog, "smell. But Miss Mildred can never resist a hopeless cause, so I guess we're stuck with you. Well, I hope you're happy, dog. It's thanks to you that my garden club party was the party to end all parties."

The party to end all parties, thought Kit. *Oh dear.*

After Kit and Aunt Millie cleaned up the party mess, they bathed and fed the dog. Then they went upstairs to the attic together. Kit brought the dog along. She was afraid to let the dog out of her sight for fear of what the animal might do! Of course, the dog looked sweetly peaceful and serene now. It rested its head on Kit's knee and looked up at Kit with trusting, loving eyes.

"Aunt Millie," said Kit, "I'm sorry the dog ruined the party."

"Nothing was broken," said Aunt Millie. "And the ladies had already eaten all the refreshments, so nothing was wasted. The dog just provided a rather spectacular ending to the party."

"Mother said it was the party to end all parties," said Kit. She sighed deeply.

"There now, Margaret Mildred," Aunt Millie said. "'Sigh no more,' as Shakespeare would say. Tell me what's on your mind."

Kit went to her desk and took the picture of the Robin Hood birthday party out of the drawer. She showed it to Aunt Millie. "I really wanted a birthday party this year," she said. "I knew it couldn't be as fancy as the one in this picture, and I probably shouldn't want one at all. But Stirling and Ruthie said that wanting was the same as hoping, and that hope is always good." Kit sighed again, in spite of Shakespeare. "They were wrong. After what happened today, there's absolutely no chance that there will be any party for me. I was stupid to hope."

"Well!" said Aunt Millie crisply. "I happen to agree with Ruthie and Stirling. I hate to give up on *anything*. Not hopes, not parties . . ." She smiled. "Not even a homely creature like this dog you found who trips over her own feet and causes all kinds of trouble!"

45

Aunt Millie's words made Kit feel better. She hugged the dog. "What should I call her?" she asked.

"There's only one name for a dog as clumsy and ungraceful as that," said Aunt Millie.

"What is it?" asked Kit.

"Grace," said Aunt Millie.

So Grace it was.

PENNY-PINCHER PARTY

It seemed, after all, that Grace had only been trying to express how happy she was to meet the chickens. Much to everyone's surprise, Grace soon became the chickens' best friend. She followed Kit around when Kit fed the chickens, and spent most of her day asleep outside their coop. That was just as well, because there she was out of Mother's sight. Whenever Kit came outside to be sure the chickens had enough water, Grace opened one eye, thumped her tail lazily, then went back to sleep. The chickens forgave and accepted Grace. They went about the business of eating their feed, clucking, and laying their eggs with Grace for company.

"These chickens are the fattest and finest chickens in Cincinnati," Aunt Millie said one day when she and Kit were feeding them.

"They should be," said Kit, folding up an empty feed sack, "considering all the feed they eat." Kit didn't mean to sound critical of the chickens. She still liked *them* even if she did dislike selling their eggs.

"I'll take that feed sack," said Aunt Millie. "I have something special in mind for it."

I wonder what? thought Kit as she handed Aunt Millie the big, flowered sack. *Dish towels? Pillowcases? No matter what, it'll be something new for the "Sewing" section of* **Aunt Millie's Waste-Not, Want-Not Almanac!**

All of the sections of the *Almanac* were more and more filled in. Kit, Ruthie, and Stirling had carefully recorded Aunt Millie's recipe for pickling "dilly beans," the early green beans from the vegetable patch. They'd also written her advice about storing winter woolen blankets and coats in mothballs for the summer. How Kit wished she could put away her winter woolen school clothes, too! But her spring clothes from last year did not fit

her, and there was no money to buy new clothes.
So, despite the fact that the weather was growing
warmer, Kit had to wear heavy, uncomfortable
winter clothes to school. As soon as she came home
to work in the garden, she put on the raggy, baggy
old overalls she had inherited from Charlie. When
Kit kicked off her shoes and peeled off her socks and
worked barefoot in the vegetable patch, she felt like
a different person—one her classmates wouldn't
even recognize.

The day before Kit's birthday was the warmest
day yet. Kit could feel sweat prickling the back of
her neck under her wool collar as she walked to
school with Stirling and Ruthie, and it was only
eight o'clock in the morning!

By afternoon Kit's clothes felt so tight and
itchy that she could hardly pay attention
to her teacher, Mr. Fisher. The classroom
was stuffy even with the windows open,
and everyone else seemed restless, too.
The students all wiggled in their seats. There
was lots of whispering and foot shuffling.

"Boys and girls!" Mr. Fisher said sharply.
"Quiet!"

At that moment, the door to the classroom swung open. The students spun around to see who it was. When they did, they stared.

Kit gasped. It was Aunt Millie!

A low ripple of giggles swept through the classroom. Kit looked at Aunt Millie through her classmates' eyes and understood why they were giggling. Aunt Millie did look peculiar. She was wearing her clean but faded workaday dress, and her Sunday-best hat and shoes. Her hair wisped out from under her hat. Her cheeks were ruddier than usual.

"Mr. Fisher," she said in her twangy voice, "I'm Margaret Mildred Kittredge's Aunt Millie, and I'd like to speak to your class."

"Uh, certainly," Mr. Fisher said. "Go ahead."

Aunt Millie beamed at Kit as she strode to the front of the classroom. Kit tried hard to smile back at Aunt Millie, but she couldn't. The classroom hissed with whispers. Roger, the boy behind Kit, poked her back. "That's your aunt?" he asked. "She looks like she just got off the farm."

Kit flushed with anger—and embarrassment. Roger was right. The way Aunt Millie looked was fine at home, but it was all wrong here in front of Kit's classmates. *Oh, why did Aunt Millie come here?* she wondered.

"I've come today to invite all of you to a birthday party for Margaret Mildred," Aunt Millie said. "It'll be after school tomorrow at our house, and it'll be a jim-dandy."

Jim-dandy? Some of the students laughed and repeated Aunt Millie's unfamiliar expression to one another in giggled whispers.

This is terrible, thought Kit. She stiffened as Aunt Millie went on. "I've been teaching Margaret Mildred and her friends lots of ways to save money and have fun at the same time," Aunt Millie said. "They've enjoyed it, and I bet all of you would, too. So come to our Penny-Pincher Party tomorrow. You can have beans out of our vegetable patch. I'll show you how to make a salad out of dandelion greens, and you can feed the chickens."

Chickens! The students exploded in merriment. They flapped their arms as if they were chicken wings. Some of the girls and boys made clucking sounds, and Roger crowed like a rooster.

Kit was so mortified she wished she could

disappear and never be seen again. But Aunt Millie
did not seem the least bit disturbed by the students'
antics. "I'll even show you how to make bloomers
out of a flour sack!" she said.

Bloomers! Now the students were laughing out
loud. Aunt Millie laughed, too, as if they were all in
on a wonderful joke together.

She doesn't even realize they are making fun of her!
Kit thought. *She doesn't know that now they will make
fun of* ***me.*** *Oh, how I wish she had never come!* Kit
thought of how she'd felt at the grocery store, and
selling the eggs. *It was bad enough to be embarrassed*

in front of strangers. This is much, much worse.

"Well!" said Mr. Fisher to Aunt Millie. "Thank you!" He turned to Kit. "Perhaps you'd like to escort your aunt to the door," he said.

Kit stood up. Her knees were wobbly, and she was so red in the face, she felt as if she were on fire. Silently, she led Aunt Millie through the halls to the front door of the school.

"Margaret Mildred," asked Aunt Millie, "whatever is the matter?"

Kit bit her lip and looked at her shoes. She was too angry to look Aunt Millie in the eyes.

"Don't you *like* the idea of the Penny-Pincher Party?" Aunt Millie asked.

"No," said Kit in a raspy whisper. She looked up at Aunt Millie with eyes that were full of hot tears. "I don't. I hate it. It's . . . *embarrassing*. Why did you tell everyone at school about the things we do at home? That's private. I don't want my friends to know how poor we are. I never want them to *see* it. Oh, I wish . . . I wish you had never come!"

Aunt Millie stepped back. "Ah," she said softly. "I see." She turned away from Kit. "I'm sorry, dear child," she said. Then she left.

Kit, Ruthie, and Stirling did not talk as they walked home together after school. As soon as Kit got to her house, she ran upstairs to her room and flung herself face-down on her bed. All the burning tears she had bottled up inside came pouring out. Kit cried and cried. Soon her pillow was hot and damp from her tears and her sweat.

A soothing breeze blew in the window and lifted the hair stuck to the back of Kit's neck. Kit raised her head so that the breeze could cool her face. Suddenly, she sat up. Hanging in front of the window, fluttering gently on the breeze, was a dress. It was simple and flowery, springy and *beautiful*. Kit stood up, pulled off her too-heavy winter clothes, and slipped the dress on. It felt so cool and light and airy, she felt as if she could fly. Kit smoothed the front of the dress with her hands and looked at the material. It was then that she realized: the dress was made out of a chicken-feed sack. It was another one of Aunt Millie's magical transformations.

Kit sat down hard on the bed. *Oh, Aunt Millie!* she thought. *How could I have spoken to you the way I did at school? How could I have been ashamed of you? How could I have been so wrong?*

Kit ran downstairs as fast as she could and found Mother and Dad in the kitchen. "Where's Aunt Millie?" she asked.

"Kit, sweetheart, Aunt Millie asked us to say good-bye to you for her," said Dad. "She decided to go home on the four-thirty train today."

"She's *gone*?" wailed Kit. "Oh, it's all my fault." Hurriedly, Kit told Mother and Dad what had happened at school. "But now I see how wrong I was. Please, we've got to stop her. You don't want her to go back to Kentucky, do you?"

Dad looked at Mother with a question in his eyes. Suddenly, Mother smiled. "If we hurry," she said, "we can catch her before she gets on the train."

The train station was huge, noisy, and full of people. But Kit spotted Aunt Millie right away. She was sitting perfectly straight with her suitcase by her side, reading a book of Shakespeare's poems. Kit ran to her.

"Aunt Millie!" Kit said breathlessly.

Cincinnati's train station

"I'm so sorry! Please don't go."

Mother and Dad came up behind Kit. "We need you, Miss Mildred," said Mother. "We can't get along without you."

"Won't you come back with us?" asked Dad.

Aunt Millie smiled a small smile. "No, my dears," she said. "You've been very kind, putting up with me and my bossiness. But I can see that my country ways don't fit here in the city. For you they are . . ." She gave Kit a kindly, forgiving look, then said, "For you they are embarrassing." Then she spoke briskly. "No, it's time for me to go, and take my ideas with me."

Kit sat down next to Aunt Millie. Gently, she took Aunt Millie's book out of her hands and put another book in its place. It was the *Waste-Not, Want-Not Almanac.* "Look," Kit said earnestly, turning the pages so that Aunt Millie could see. "Stirling and Ruthie and I made this. It's full of your ideas. We liked them so much, we put them in this book so we'd never forget them."

"Hea-ven-ly day!" said Aunt Millie in a long, drawn out, surprised whisper. She touched the dandelion green Ruthie had glued to a page, studied

*"Look," Kit said earnestly, turning the pages so that Aunt Millie could see.
"Stirling and Ruthie and I made this."*

Stirling's sketch of the chickens, and smiled at Kit's list of grocery shopping tips. When she looked up at Kit, Mother, and Dad, her eyes were bright.

"I hope you'll come home, Aunt Millie," said Kit, "and teach all my friends your ideas, too, at the Penny-Pincher Party."

Aunt Millie stood up and held out her hand to Kit. "'Let's away,'" she said, quoting Shakespeare in her old, lively way.

Dad carried her suitcase and Mother carried her basket, because Aunt Millie's hands were full. She was holding Kit's hand in one of her hands, and carrying the *Waste-Not, Want-Not Almanac* in the other.

The Penny-Pincher Party was the best birthday party Kit had ever had. Kit's classmates agreed afterward that it was the best birthday party *anyone* had ever had.

Aunt Millie had planned the whole party, but everyone helped. Stirling made paper party hats for all the guests, including Grace, who appeared to be under the impression that the party was in *her* honor. She trotted from guest to guest and leaned up against each one, allowing the chance to pet her. While Mr. Peck played his bass fiddle, Mr. and Mrs. Bell taught the children to square-dance and Miss Hart and Miss Finney taught them to sing "My Darling Clementine." The ragman was there, and he and Dad gave the children rides on his horse. Charlie took pictures of them with his camera. Aunt Millie's friend the butcher helped the children cook hot dogs on sticks over a fire, and Mrs. Howard and Mother taught the children to make flower crowns and necklaces.

The children liked Aunt Millie's penny-pincher lessons best of all. Aunt Millie taught them how to pick the most tender dandelion greens to make a salad. She showed them how to feed the chickens and collect their eggs. She brought out a flour sack full of sunflower seeds and taught the children how to plant, water, and weed. "Remember," she said, quoting Shakespeare, "'sweet flowers take time, weeds make haste.'"

When the flour sack was empty, Aunt Millie held it up. "Well," she said, with a twinkle in her eye.

"Look at this. An empty cloth sack. Would you like me to show you how to make bloomers out of this?"

"Yes!" shouted all the children, including Kit. They laughed, and Kit realized that even in school, they had been laughing in delight at the idea, not meanly. They were as enchanted by Aunt Millie as Kit and Stirling and Ruthie had been.

"You are so lucky, Kit," sighed Ruthie. "This is a wonderful party." The sun had set. The yard was lit with lanterns Aunt Millie had saved from a trash pile and repaired. The lanterns had candles inside them, and they swayed in the soft evening breeze so that their light danced across the grass. Kit, Ruthie, and Stirling were sitting together eating the chocolate roll cake Aunt Millie had made. Ruthie asked, "Do you mind that it's not a Robin Hood party?"

"You know, in a way it *is* a Robin Hood party," Kit said, "because Aunt Millie reminds me of Robin Hood. She doesn't rob from the rich to give to the poor. But she scrimps and saves and then whatever she has, she gives away. She's thrifty in order to be generous." Kit spread out her arms. "Look at this party she's created for all of us, even after I was terrible to her about it."

"How *did* you convince her not to leave?" asked Stirling.

Kit grinned. "How do you think?" she asked.

Ruthie and Stirling both looked at Kit with sparkling eyes. "You showed her the *Almanac*!" they said together.

"Yup," said Kit, *"Aunt Millie's Waste-Not, Want-Not Almanac*, with all her great ideas inside."

"You know," said Stirling, "I think we should add a new section."

"Right!" said Ruthie. "We could call it 'Having a Penny-Pincher Party.'"

"Or maybe," said Kit, "'How to Have a Very Happy Birthday.'"

Looking
Back
1934

A PEEK INTO
THE PAST

In the 1930s, when girls like Kit were growing up, most babies were born at home. Doctors usually came to the home and helped the mother while the rest of the family waited in another room. Larger cities had hospitals, but many families during the Great Depression couldn't afford a hospital stay. Finding money to pay for even a home delivery was a challenge. Doctors sometimes received food or services, such as carpentry work, in exchange for delivering a baby.

As more and more people lost their jobs and homes because of the Depression, families had fewer children. Some people were so upset by the terrible conditions created by the Depression that they felt it was unfair to bring children into such a harsh world. Other people just couldn't afford to have children.

These twin boys were separated soon after this photo was taken because their parents could not afford to raise two babies.

64

This couple kept their 1932 marriage a secret for three years so that the wife wouldn't lose her job. Although married, she continued to live with and support her parents.

Fewer people were getting married, too. Couples couldn't afford to set up their own households, and many working women who married were fired so that single women or men with families could have their jobs. Instead of marrying, many young people stayed at home to contribute to their parents' households.

During these dark days, some men *deserted*, or abandoned, their families, as Stirling's father did. Many men left home to find new jobs elsewhere and send money back to their families until they could come home. But some men were so ashamed of losing their jobs and not being able to support their families that they never came back. Others left because they thought their families would be able to get government help more easily with no man at home.

Many men ended up traveling around the country, looking for work wherever they could find it.

Children helped their parents grow and preserve fruits and vegetables for winter.

Families changed in other ways, too. Households expanded as relatives and even friends moved in together to save money. Everyone pitched in to make ends meet. Children often took over household chores while their parents worked—or looked for work. Girls like Kit did laundry, cooked, cleaned, and cared for younger children. Boys sold newspapers and worked at odd jobs. Women like Kit's mother and Aunt Millie found many small ways to save money and stretch what they had. They bought day-old bread and cheaper cuts of meat. They ironed on the days they baked, saving money by heating the iron on the hot stove instead of with electricity. They planted vegetable gardens and, even in the city, kept cows and chickens for milk, meat, and eggs.

Some farm families survived the Depression better than city families, mainly because farm families could grow more of their own food. Even if they couldn't afford electricity and indoor plumbing, they had food to eat and trade for other things they needed.

This whole family worked together to make apple cider.

Feed-sack fashions

During the Depression—long before the word *recycle* was ever used—people saved or recycled everything. Their motto was, "Use it up, wear it out, make it do, or do without." Mothers cut up their old clothes to make clothing for their children. They turned coats inside out and resewed them to make them look new. They turned worn-out clothes into quilts, braided rugs, or cleaning rags, or sold them to a ragman for a few cents.

Women even made use of the cloth sacks that flour and animal feed came in. Flour sacks became dish towels and underwear. Animal feed sacks printed in colorful floral or geometric patterns became aprons, pajamas, doll clothes, or dresses like the one Aunt Millie made for Kit. One woman said, "A ten-pound flour bag was a pair of training pants for the baby. I never bought five pounds of anything because you got that in a paper bag, and I didn't have any use for a paper bag."

Doll clothes made from feed sacks

67

A doctor examining children for tuberculosis

Although people were resourceful, many often went hungry. Some children growing up during the Depression suffered from rickets and other diseases caused by poor nutrition. Diseases like scarlet fever, whooping cough, influenza, and tuberculosis were dangerous even to healthy children, but undernourished children had a harder time fighting these illnesses. Polio, a serious threat during the 1920s, continued to attack both children and adults in the 1930s. In fact, the new president, Franklin Roosevelt, could not walk without canes because he was partly paralyzed by polio.

Many people felt that Roosevelt understood the suffering because of his own battle with polio.

After Roosevelt became president in 1933, new government programs started to provide jobs and relief from the Depression. But in spite of these programs and the additional jobs that they created, many families continued to struggle.

People did find ways to cope with the hard times and have fun with little money. Everyone read more—library books were free, and libraries offered a quiet escape from the hardships of the

Roosevelt's Works Progress Administration created new jobs.

Bookmobiles brought books to people who lived far from a library.

Depression. Many families grew closer because they spent more time at home together. Jigsaw puzzles, card games, and board games were popular. People saved their nickels to see the latest comedies, musicals, or gangster movies. More than anything else, though, Americans listened to the radio. In addition to news, comedy, mystery, and drama, the radio brought President Roosevelt's broadcasts to the American people, called "fireside chats," into their homes—and renewed hope that the Depression would eventually end.

Movie theaters were crowded on "dish night," when people got a free plate or bowl with their ticket.

Families gathered around the radio to enjoy programs such as **Adventure Time with Orphan Annie.**

THE BOOKS ABOUT KIT

MEET KIT ◆ An American Girl
Kit Kittredge and her family get news that
turns their household upside down.

KIT LEARNS A LESSON ◆ A School Story
It's Thanksgiving, and Kit learns a surprising
lesson about being thankful.

KIT'S SURPRISE ◆ A Christmas Story
The Kittredges may lose their house.
Can Kit still find a way to make Christmas
merry and bright for her family?

HAPPY BIRTHDAY, KIT! ◆ A Springtime Story
Kit loves Aunt Millie's thrifty ideas—until Aunt Millie
plans a pinch-penny party and invites Kit's whole class.

KIT SAVES THE DAY ◆ A Summer Story
Kit's curiosity and longing for adventure
lead her to unexpected places—and into trouble!

CHANGES FOR KIT ◆ A Winter Story
Kit writes a letter that brings changes and
new hope—in spite of the hard times.

◆

WELCOME TO KIT'S WORLD ◆ 1934
American history is lavishly portrayed
with photographs, illustrations, and
excerpts from real girls' letters and diaries.